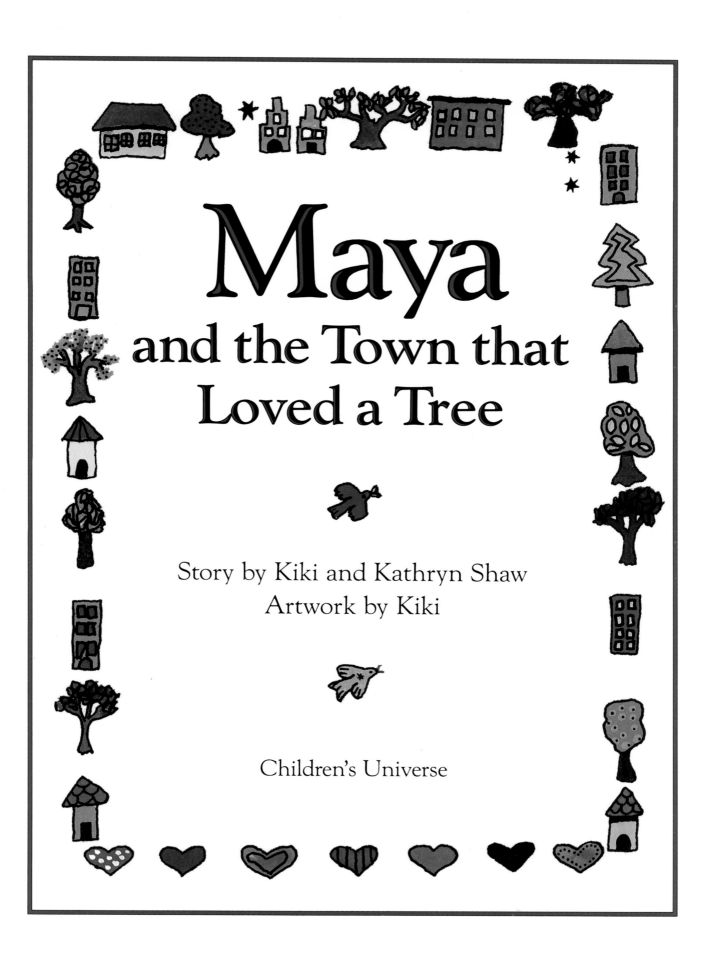

Maya
and the Town that Loved a Tree

Story by Kiki and Kathryn Shaw
Artwork by Kiki

Children's Universe

Once upon a time, in a place not so very far away, there was a little town that was a very beautiful place to live. The people were happy and friendly. They would wave to each other from their front porches and smile when they passed on the street.

The houses were painted bright colors and had pretty yards filled with flowers. There was a bakery always filled with good smells and a row of stores where the people loved to meet. There were trees everywhere in the town and the people loved to walk in the shade of their branches. They would listen to the birds sing overhead and smell the blossoms on the trees in the springtime. The green parks were always filled with children laughing and playing.

The town was such a wonderful place that people came from all over to live there.

The town grew and grew. It grew from a little town into a big town and from a big town into a big city.

The people who came brought their cars and trucks. Skyscrapers replaced the colorful little houses, shopping centers replaced the bakery and the row of shops, and factories were built all around.

As the days and years passed, highways, parking lots and tall buildings took over all the green spaces. There was so much traffic and noise you couldn't hear the birds sing or the wind whistling in the trees' branches.

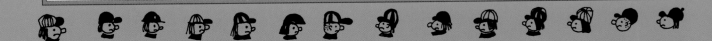

B ut the people didn't care. The changes happened slowly, and the people were too busy working and driving from place to place to notice how dull and grey their city had become.

The people, too, became dull and grey. Their faces didn't shine with happiness anymore. They didn't smile when they passed each other on the street. They became as sad and as dull as the sky above them and the city around them.

The trees were getting grey and dirty, too, but no one noticed. Trees need clean air to breathe, but with all the fumes from the traffic and factory smoke, the air was filthy. The trees felt as if they had been forgotten. They saw that the people were worried about getting from here to there, but not about the trees that they passed along the way.

The trees were sad and knew that they no longer had a place in the city. Slowly, they lost their color, then they lost their leaves. Finally, they died.

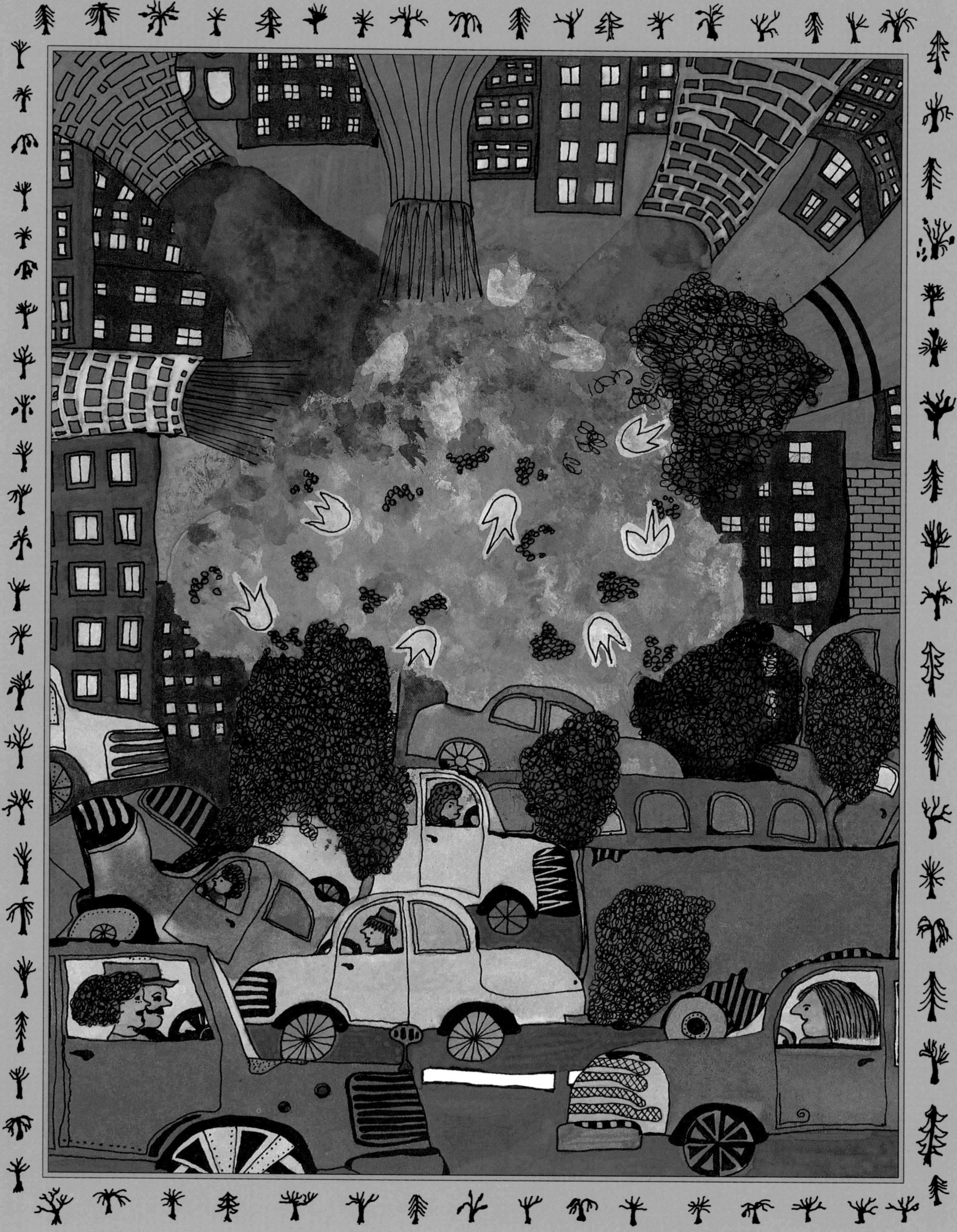

People began to stay indoors most of the time. If they missed the singing of the birds, they just turned up their radios. If their hearts became sad because their city was dreary, they turned on the TV so that they didn't have to think.

The situation had become very serious. Some scientists explained that trees are very important because their leaves help to take carbon dioxide out of the air and give us oxygen to breathe. The story was discussed on television and in the newspapers.

For the first time in ages, people looked out their windows. They looked up over their heads. The trees were all gone!

The people longed for the way things used to be. At night in their sleep, they dreamed about the beautiful green fullness of the trees, and the bright sun shining in the blue sky. They dreamed of birds singing and flowers growing. But they always awoke to a dull, grey morning.

The scientists and the government worked hard to plant trees and keep them alive, but the trees died as soon as they were planted. There was nothing anyone could do.

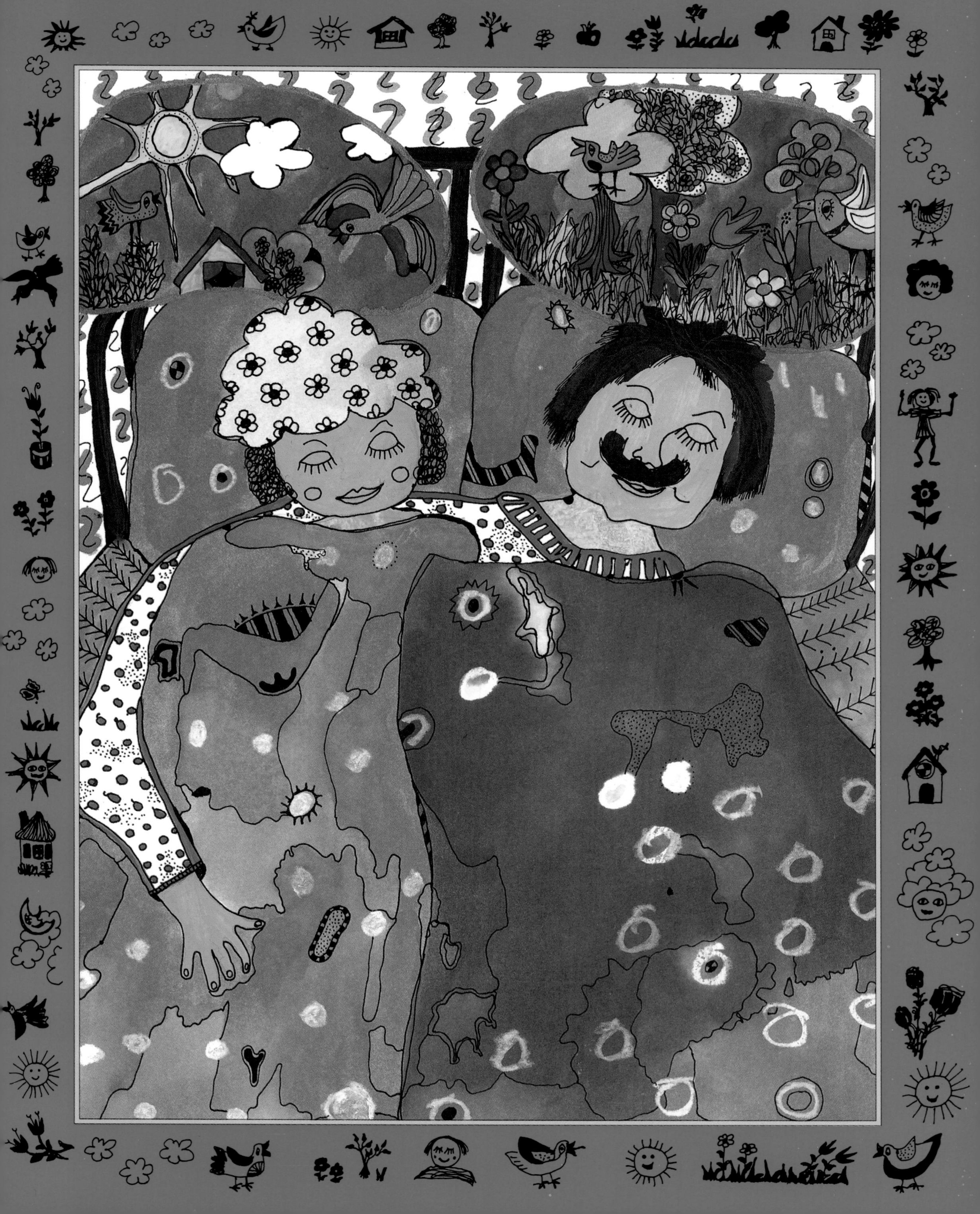

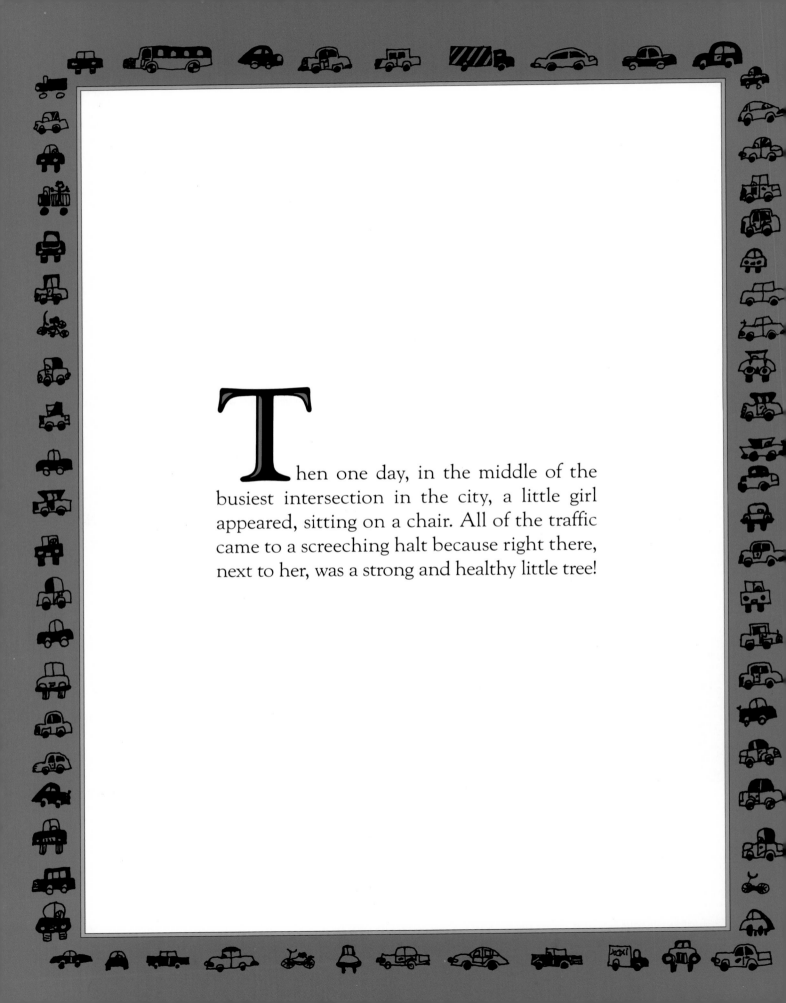

T hen one day, in the middle of the busiest intersection in the city, a little girl appeared, sitting on a chair. All of the traffic came to a screeching halt because right there, next to her, was a strong and healthy little tree!

Soon the girl and her tree were surrounded by a big crowd. There were reporters asking questions and photographers snapping pictures. No one knew who she was or from where she came. And no one could even imagine where the girl had found the wonderful, healthy tree.

Finally the girl spoke to the people. "My name is Maya," she said. "I heard that you lost all of your trees, so I will share my tree with you, but on two conditions."

"What?" the mayor said. "We will do anything you ask!"

"Well," Maya replied, "it's very simple. You must promise . . ."

"Yes?" The crowd moved in to hear.

"You must promise to work together to clean up your city and your air. And, most importantly, you must promise to love my tree!"

E veryone agreed.

The busy intersection became an island for Maya's tree. The city people carefully transplanted the tree from its pot into the ground. They planted some flowers and some grass, too.

Maya became the official city gardener. Every day she spent many hours watering her tree and sitting with it.

The people wanted their city to be clean and green, with good air for trees. So they began to pick up all the garbage and recycled all that they could. They worked to get the factories to clean up their smoke. They walked or took buses instead of driving cars everywhere they went.

They came to visit Maya and her tree. They loved her tree.

Maya's tree became strong and healthy. Lots of people came to visit, so the tree's island was made into a beautiful park with benches and a playground so everyone could enjoy the tree's shade. Then a wonderful thing happened. As people sat or played in the park, their faces grew full of color again. They were so happy to be near a green tree, smelling its fresh smell.

And the more happiness that radiated from the people's faces, the faster the tree grew. Maya's little tree became a mighty tree. In the summer, lush green leaves filled its branches. In the autumn, the leaves turned a brilliant blaze of bright color. In the winter, the tree's empty branches reminded the people of their promise to keep their city a place where trees like to live.

Maya's tree grew and grew and soon it was bigger than the tallest skyscraper. Hundreds of birds lived in its branches, big birds and little birds, of every kind and color. The tree was a glorious tree, and everyone loved it very much.

But the government officials were concerned about the tree's size and they came to Maya to talk. It was just too big, and its roots were disrupting the foundations of the buildings as well as the subways and the sewers.

Maya looked up, up to the top of her tree, way up in the sky. "You are right," she told them. "Here is what we can do: our tree won't have to grow any more, if we take its fruits and plant them. They will grow into trees to help keep the air clean and the streets shaded."

So, in the spring, the children came, from every part of the city, and each took a fruit from the great tree. They planted the fruit and many green trees sprung up all over the city. The children sat by the new little trees, and talked to them and hugged them. They loved their trees.

People continued to work hard to keep the city clean. The air became clear again. They painted their houses bright colors, planted grass and flowers everywhere, and hung baskets of bright flowers from their balconies. They had festivals in the streets and picnics in the parks.

The people were happy again, and the city was a very beautiful place to live.

I heard the story of Maya's tree during one of my many journeys and I went to the city to see it. Underneath its spread of branches, I found Maya! I sat down beside her and told her about the cities I had visited in many different lands as well as those in my own country which were getting greyer and dirtier every day.

There was hope in her eyes when she said, "You must tell the story of this tree to as many people as you can. They must avoid the mistakes that were made here."

We talked for awhile beneath the clear skies, and then it was time for me to go. As I reached the gate of the park, I heard Maya call my name. I turned and saw her waving to me. As she waved, she said, "Tell the story to the children! Especially, tell it to the children!"

To Katharina

First published in the United States of America in 1992 by
Children's Universe
Rizzoli International Publications, Inc.
300 Park Avenue South, New York, New York 10010

Cataloging-in-Publication Data for this book is available
from the Library of Congress.

92 93 94 95 96 / 10 9 8 7 6 5 4 3 2 1

Cover and book design by Charles Kreloff
Printed in Hong Kong